About the Author

Jia Olympia graduated Bachelor of Secondary Education major in English and took up units of Creative Writing course in her Master's.

She has been an instructor teaching Creative and Creative Nonfiction Writing to Senior High School Humanities and Social Sciences students in her home country Cebu, Philippines.

She is now an international student studying Early Childhood Education and Care in Sydney, Australia while pursuing her dreams of becoming an author.

MONOLOQUY:

Inner Voices of Poetry

Jia Olympia
©2020

*I*ntroduction

Have you ever heard the sound of your
voice whispering, pushing you toward
the ravine of blazing words? What's its
sound like?

Happy?

In love?

Angry?

Thirsty of Revenge?

Is it sane? Or shouting like insane?

Is it child-like? Or matured-type?

Monoloquy: Poetry of Inner Voices is a
collection of poetry written in different
forms: villanelle, haiku, and mostly free
verse. The writer used her poetic license
of generating a newly formed word to
design a symbolism of her thoughts
performing in the reader's mind.
Monoloquy,   a blended word

composed of monologue and soliloquy.
Both monologue and soliloquy are
terms in drama, particularly in theatre
play, involving a solitary speaker
addressing speech to the audience or to
one's self. Therefore,   Monoloquy:
Poetry of inner Voices was written to
actualise the writer's venture to execute
scenes as if watching an actual play but
just only in a form of poetry. It permits
them to join the writer in her walks of
life, encounters and imagination, and
together, see her own interpretation of
varied experiences that do not confine
only to one single individual and allows
them to criticise it at their own pace.
According to a quote, "some things are
better left unsaid." Thence, it paved the
way for the writer to view reader's mind
as stage to perform her inner thoughts
and voices of joy, excitement, boredom,
disappointments, grief, dreams and
aspirations, and to present various faces

of love and the writer's quest of love
and admirations through
poetry.Common denominator among all
poems is love which is illustrated in
various shapes disclosing the drawbacks
of excessive, bizarre, self-centered love
and featuring a taste of multicultural
connection, their resiliency towards
differences and judgments.

Titles & Content

"Writing is the body of one's soul.

It makes one's thoughts to be seen.
Otherwise, the latter may fall as just the lost
soul."

~ Jia Olympia

for
My Family & Friends

21*st* Century Invaders

The land invasion has been ceased,
At rest the Kings and Queens on throne.
If not, in peaceful sense at least,
although break-ins sometimes be seen in
  zone.

But what remains the remnants of this
  war,
is strife of mind between the dripping
  blood
from fountain, roots are cut in part
Detached its tenets, crushed, soul flood.

How trepid, how creepy this wave is!
They come in groups, & braver those
    alone.
Contemporary sorcery kins of kins,
no doll, not poppit shown being sewn.

No arms of guns with bullets and
bombs,
but noise so loud, ear-shattering sound.
Invaded wit covered by palms,
no mark, no trace, but scars that hound.

And when this poisoned sound on
    board,
it feeds on truth demands dispute.
Toxic travels through unfigured chord,
enjoying ruins of blocked pursuit.

Cheers to the Old Wise Flower

Cheers to the old wise Flower!
held by Bee, as old as Her shadow.
Gasping, as the Queen elevates Her
    tower.
Lethargic petals like the sunset of
    yellow.

His wings converged, stuck unto her
Vanished mortality to caress her thorn.
Til' time turns whole of its hour.
No minute shall pass in every second
    born.

Cheers to the old wise Flower!
Before its parts depart its whole,
before the sun looses her raging fire
before the magma stops rising from
    core.

Monoloquy: Poetry of Inner Voices

Her petals crease of yesterdays gleam.
Hurricane - tiny bits shadow of soil,
yet worth fuels its roots to fill, rooted
    firm
pollen ground till new sprout spill.

Crimson and Gold Feathers

Gagged our wings coated resentments,
chained, shuddered turbulence.
Key, in clouds, hides underneath,
seeking down the heath.

When sun shattered, supernova sprouted.
Million feathers among scattered.
Fascinated! How brilliant! How light!
Our feathers, with all these we fight.

I wept, you cried, 'til it went dry,
You stroke my wing, we flew up high.
Ignites the hope, no match can light.
This tie that binds, no loose nor tight..

Broken standards, conquered petrifaction,
flaunting feathers with genuine passion,
cautious! what those eyes might say,
Fly still and let them be, let them be!

Arduous journey has been made,
None of our feathers did fade,
Feathers of crimson and gold,
This story will never be old.

Foreign Dishes

Two tongues speak foreign dishes -
which of which must be eaten?
In the banquet of such prospect.
where two beliefs intersecting.
Intimate blood guests from two flags.
This small trouble is a dessert,
since banana and strawberry,
would always taste good together.
They speak, "Hakuna Matata!"
"Love is so strong, it won't go wrong!"
Strong as the tides are up high
Waves reaching the impossible
Rifts created by hundreds of years,
tremors and shambles of wounded.
Clock is past due, healed and it's time,
different strings tied, links as one.
The couple are polar regions,
opposite yet, they are stable.

Their union is the world's treaty,
sanctified,
a peace offering,
for saints who fought with their hearts
smiled.
Divided by oceans,
yet colours,well-blended.
Something can be made prettily,
from the things hopeless they may seem,
As miraculously sightly,
As the couple standing above,
Above the sea of scornful slurs,
still they shine, glimmering hope
Someday, the taboo turns truth.

*G*ray

Lovely, you are, what more can I say?
Just can't look straight into your eyes
My dream is to hold you and say you're my
    gray.

Something in you captures my every day
Raging fire in your eyes that hides
Lovely, you are, what more can I say?

You are the earth, I am the moon, I say.
Your gravity keeps our ties.
My dream is to hold you and say you're my
    gray.

Your smile as gold as the crepuscule sunny
    day
that brings the blaze in me that never die.
Lovely, you are, what more can I say?

Whenever I see you my nerves go fray,
then gapes insanely, look at skies -
My dream is to hold you and say you're my
    gray.

Heart may be blind, but not crippled, I say
It can reach a thousand miles
Lovely, you are, what more can I say?
My dream is to hold you and say you're my
    gray.

Monoloquy: Poetry of Inner Voices

GUILTY!

You kept your windows opened.

You kept the beam imbalanced.

You kept justice under wild.

You kept your treatment unfair.

You kept your shallow eyes.

Intractable wrath.

You keep this floor, for now.

Take note, the wheel is round.

One day, you'll see,

my fiery indignation.

I Dropped My Sole to Goldland

I dropped my sole to Goldland -
welcomed me as grandiose as the rising
    sun.
Scent of perfume gold dust -
I sniffed - I dreamt, with eyes open
how gentle, how bizarre!
This flavour of gold stained my old
    mine.

I dropped my sole to Goldland.
with four quadrants of sphere in arrow
where skin be bold and gold
then flowers dead
covered in cold
and rise like it never falls.

Monoloquy: Poetry of Inner Voices

I dropped my sole to Goldland
to fill my hands with gold
knees bent like candy cane
my feet soaked, buried
in the sand dunes of rust.

I sold my soul to Goldland
To dig gems other than mine
Sapphire, opal, jade and pearls
more than gold, diamonds, I reap
to free my blood whose eyes deceived.

I Have a Terrible Accent

I have a *tiribol* accent, yes me.
but know to spill *tiribol*, don't me.
t.e. double r, i, b, l, e as in eagle with e
See? I know how to spill. I studied hard,
     hillo.
but still my people laugh at me you know.

Jus' like how I pronounce my country
     /pelepens/
My titser Mrs. dickhens told me to follow her
     hands
She said /fi/ I gave her /fi/
She said /li/ I gave her /li/
She said /pins/ I gave her /pins/
Ok Purification, are you ready?
Yes mam, I was born ready!
/filipins/, /pelefens/
/fi---lipins/, /fi--lefens/
/fi--li--pins/, /fi--li--fens/

Philippines *Tonto*! Now, go back to seat!
My furious titser pointed her short stick,

on the blackboard which I always called green
    board
'coz all the blackboard in my school was
    green,
are you all bored?
It's not only me who was stupid, you see.
All my classmates were,
Including my titser, Mrs. Dickens,
Can't you see?

Back in high school, I graduated almost a
    Salutatorian.
Ofcourse, I am victorian in the Pearl of the
    Orient.
I don't know, I always won *pers* in
    everything,
smells fishy, isn't it a thing?
Feature writing, editorial writing, news
    writing,
technical writing, creative writing,
singing, dancing except *por* reading &
    public speaking.
That is a bull of a sheet of paper,
wool of the sheep
horn of a jeepney beep, beep, beep.

I knew I did great in *diclamition*,
What's wrong with my *pronouncition?*
Any *objiction, siliction, incantition?*
Are you judge to perform the *justificition?*
   Even in real acting *jus'* when the director
     said the queuing -
cry in one, two, three, I started crying.
Jus' at the start when I *great* everyone,
     from my diaphram
"*Lidis en gintilmen* good afternoon all"

The school applauded me whole,
yelled at me, calling me
"*idoooooool,*"
It boosted my confidence, I knew I
     would make sense,
"Alms, alms," I looked at the people,
     they started to cry.
Good thing I listened to Mam Helen
     Grace Cruz not to cry,
but to use just my voice to make people
     cry.
Then followed, "/spir me a peace of
     brid, spir me your mersi/
"Alms, alms."

Monoloquy: Poetry of Inner Voices

I glanced at Mam Cruz, she bowed her
    head,
she put her hand on her forehead,
thought she had an aching head.
She was more nervous than I did.
She was touched, I think.
So as my fellow students,
I gave them heart attack, I think.
at the end of my piece, I said it again,
"Alms, alms" *spir me a peace of brid, spir me
    your mercy."*
Everybody got teary red eyes,
how could I forget the day
just when the time announced the winner,
    yes!
"Congratulations to the non-winner
"Purificacion Pelaez!"
"Please dont' lose hope joining this
    contest.
I was in terrible shock whispering
    electromagnetic block,
facing hollow block, all I saw was black.
Because of that, didn't snatch valedictorian
    slot.
Not just that,
to be honest to my entire ancestral blood

living under hut
It was the grand finals, the public speaking
When I heard my co-debator saying,

> *"Perhaps the labor party would give*
> *all those things up, easily.*
> *Perhaps they would agree to a single*
> *currency*
> *to total abolition of the pound*
> *sterling.*
> *Perhaps being totally incompetent*
> *with monetary matters,*
> *they'd be only too delighted to hand*
> *over*
> *the full responsibility as they did to the*
> *IMF, to a central bank."*

"OMG, what an accent with t,
but wait a minute,
let me grab a piece of cake with tea.
Did we have a pound sterling in my
     country?
Did she hide that in her panty?
So twas the day of graduation,
the most important day in our nation,

another wave of youth building the
    federation,
I had to speak my salutatory speech,
it was brief.
Shorter than gettysburg address speech,
but no grief
Then I started my speech by greeting
    my fellow kids.
"Students, parents, administrators, good
    morning *pips.*
I'd like to inculcate in the mindset of the
    youth of my country
That accent is the least thing to be listed
as essence of absolute intelligence.
I'll tell you in what sense;

*Yes, the Commission does want to
        increase its powers.*
Yes, it is a non-elected body and
*I do not want the Commission to increase
        its powers at the expense of the
        House,*
so of course we are differing. Of course…
*The Chairman or the president of the
        Commission, Mr. Delors,*
said at a press conference the other day

that he wanted the European Parliament
to be the democratic body of the
  Community,
he wanted the Commission to be the
  Executive
and he wanted the Council of Ministers
to be the Senate. No. No. No.
Or… or…..or…..
Perhaps the Labour party would give all
  those things up easily.
Perhaps it would agree to a   single
  currency,
to total abolition of the pound sterling.
Perhaps, being totally incompetent with
  monetary matters,
they'd be only too delighted
to hand over full responsibility
  as they did to the IMF, to a central
  bank.
  The fact is they have no competence
  on money and no competence on the
  economy——so, yes, the right hon.
  Gentleman would be glad to hand it
  all over."

Monoloquy: Poetry of Inner Voices

Yes you're right, the Valedictorian took
    her last final speech
From my *peborite* speaker's speech
with whom others treat like bird who
    screech -
United Kingdom Prime Minister
    Margaret Thatcher with high pitch.
Thief, stealer, burglar, classmate of
    mine,
now it's my time to take mine
that gold medal from Balatoc mine.
Now, tell me I had a terrible accent, I
    don't mind
Because accent is NOT everything
Just to make the people *si* "you're
    amazing"
But laugh towards the person you're
    mocking?

20

Monoloquy: Poetry of Inner Voices

You're nothing.
You might have great pronunciation,
elocution, inflection, congratulation
But a single man in possession
of a good fortune must be in want of a
    wife.
You have no connection, no
    apprehension
I have a *tiribol* accentuation but
I spoke of my valedictory speech in my
    graduation.

Monoloquy: Poetry of Inner Voices

In His Room

Oh! Where should I stay?
And where should I hide,
if storm will come today?
Will I ever live and survive?
Hunger and Famine await,
and my resources are few.
In the storm, I may, be bait,
As far as I can, I must go through.
Man alone is helpless,
but if his life will never subdue,
he must collect his memories,
and to God he must move.
If ever, I will be in His room,
alone in storm.

Letter of an Almost Old Maid
During Corona Pandemic.

Dear future flame,

With your anxiety, I am of known.
I, too, am exhilarated. Patient, though:
to lock our palms with fingers
      pinned fraternal rings;
to whisper semantics in our ears
      even nature cannot hear;
to bind our lips with seasoned kiss;
to fill our box with crayons of gold
     which eyed our bonds untold;
to collide but not to shatter;
to argue but stick to the matter;
to align goals yet keen to head

if both wants have not met;

to shroud our hearts with burning sense

of love, respect, limitless dispense.

If till 'tis time our lines uncrossed

just know I passed this course.

But hopes and aspirations kept firm,

for they're lobster of infinite yearn.

Longing,

Jia Olympia ♥☐

Love Birds of the Time

Inseparable, rift can't be, barred.

distinct wings, one of a kind, when fly, align.

Esoteric knot, keen to divulge, my nerves at

    war.

When sun awaits the young moon, that's the

    sign -

fly, lovebirds of the time.

Thawny Frogmouth, holding cigar --

absolute master of disguise, sighed

"Rio, it is, like -- obsolete, gone too far.

Madness, it is -- absolute. Fie!"

No lovebirds of the time."

"Woof-woof," Barking Owl, on the tree,

    gnarled --

screechin', too audible, pitch so high.

"Thawny most of the time hides his tart,

best at it, causing dreary heart when lie.

But, disagree not, I can't deny."

"Love only lives in the heart of myth, Dar,

Me death is proof," Nigel the gannet replied.

"Multitudes of flight -- I eyed solitaire.

Each flight Me sorted half of Me til' die."

No such thing, lovebirds of the time.

"Myth is real in Hera's eyes -- art --
Peacock, no one's as fair as this guy.
Fame devoured his soul, with angst he bark.
stains of tears, my feathers dry
Legend -- the lovebirds of the time."

"We make love, always, her core I find blue
      star.
When she soars high, I soar high.
When she's down, I reach down afar.
My Steere's Pita, I dig worms for gems I vie
Phoenix -- the lovebirds of the time."

Monoloquy: Poetry of Inner Voices

Wrong tree, I think I bark -- birds who jarred,

devoured of grief, love must not pile.

Stained pure feather, poor leather heart --

fell off tree dried in beehive,

yet my credence remains untouched, all this

      time.

Spring has come, for glory of card

Unseen of lovebirds I must defy

Twisted faith forsaken the ward

Must I shovel the broken roots of blind

And budge them up where the sun is high.

Seas have dried, mountains dark

I got no home but the Sky

I aim to fly, keenly fly and hark

If may, unearth from clouds' mind

and find these lovebirds in time.

Monoloquy: Poetry of Inner Voices

Mystery Crush

On the other side of the glass, you are.

Walking, gently, as Boreas' power

   gloriously blows,

Stripping everything that blocks my core.

One world, same poles;

One world, twin souls, same road

But can't quite be closed.

I've seen you new but in my dreams it's

   been old.

In the corner, these windows, dancing

   grace,

gazing your highness in her velvet red coat.

Lips cherry plum of taste;

Skin so soft I want to caress;

Hands so cold I want to hold and lace.

With your name I'm Greek.

Though dreams,   we leave it best,

let it be a mystery, I cannot speak.

Monoloquy: Poetry of Inner Voices

My Box is Filled but Soul Empty

My box is filled,

But soul empty.

Perfused with fabricated lies

of mouths who screech

but barrels empty.

Charged with Boreas' skin

handed amity.

Conceived Narcissus' scheme,

speaks of enmity.

In the apogee,

muzzled folded lines

confined extremity.

May burst,

may deflate,

when clock starts wise.

Leaving my box filled,

       but soul empty.

Monoloquy: Poetry of Inner Voices

Opposite Poles

Shades embedded unto physical skin,
Like pigments outweighing in a colorful
    scheme,
Tongues of tones in its distinctive sound,
a sensation familiar for the heart to pound.

Yin and yang, balance it exemplifies.
Water and land, life it signifies.
Moon and sun shines at different times.
Yet eclipses were there for the two to align.

Hot and cold, two opposing temperatures,
Yet the extent of me's requires the presence
    you's.

Regions of continent may separate two souls,
art of language may not be an effective tool.

Complexion too unlike, as witnessed by eyes,
perspectives dissimilar, can be an open gap to
    fight.
But love, a stimulus that catalyzes wonders.
No exact definition, just a feeling felt by
    lovers.

The blind may not what the mute can see,
the mute may not what the blind could speak,
but in essence, this reaction need not senses
    be seen.
Just a pinch of life; and in this world you may
    live.

Oriental Wings

Butterfly wings,

frail and soft.

Too scared to touch,

too scared to hold.

Maybe, come a little close?

Love comes in a form of sun kissed

skin.

Smile illuminating this darkness,

Arms warm enough

  to lessen this numbness

Palm pressed on my cheeks

Lips whispering little things

that meant like everything.

Love is a far off delicacy

Pearl of the orient seas, love is

Indeed a handful of rice

When I needed spoon and fork

Love is weird.

Weird but a good kind of weird

The universe decided to abhor parallels

And banned asymptotic lines

It had to intersect

We had to meet

Like the little prince

Who had a rose of his own

There might be a lot like you

But no one's also, you

Flawlessly flawed, mine.

Monoloquy: Poetry of Inner Voices

Western Winds

Honey hued skin

Collides with snowflakes

Odd because it felt like home,

For what are the chances

That western and eastern winds meet?

Walking through traces of autumn
  sadness

Whiplash of summer madness

The blues of winter coldness

Dandelions dancing on spring, a bit
  sleepless

Its unfamiliar, but your embrace keeps
  me grounded.

It was hard till it wasn't

Distance came like a stranger

Who brought a friend named miles away

But then I remembered my middle

   name

It was, no oceans can stop this heart

You're different, I can tell

You embrace my insecurities

You kiss my flaws

I'm a shipwreck personified and you're a

   treasure hunter

I am ruined but you valued me more.

Monoloquy: Poetry of Inner Voices

It was meant to happen

I am that beautiful ending

You are that gray smile in the evening

We meet only when its time

I'm glad it is now, I'm glad you are mine.

Poisoned Island

The scent of air blended firm,

then fumes spatter then explode.

Left his island inhaled grievance of grim

'til tranquil sea never seen abode.

Its gates open, yet are closed

like an iceberg buried deep -

stiff head when bold body soaked.

Underneath are roots of frozen feet.

The waves, oh so gracious, when calm

but, how wounding when found profound.

Ruining his island of contaminated farm,

while singing with maximum sound but

bound.

Whatever it is, how wind moves hard,

the more it blows, twice its wound sound

Leaving his poor intoxicated island,

wrapped with air, suffocated then drowned.

Monoloquy: Poetry of Inner Voices

Rule Your World

Alarm strikes a quarter before time.

Get your towel, take a shower,

get dressed, at the mirror, you stare,

   deep.

At shallow holes, you gaze,

"what a lovely day!"

Alarm strikes a quarter before time,

You open your eyes.

You stretch your arms.

You feel the warmth, your skin, deep.

Shallow breath,

Legs unfold, stand uphold.

You go through windows, open

   curtains.

You see one blazing ball saying her

   "hello,"

You hear humming birds

on the trees across the road,

You taste the sweet meat of nature

and say,

"What a lovely day!"

Alarm again strikes less a quarter before

   time,

You break your fast,

get your towel,

take a shower.

You change your clothes.

You grab your shiny shoes.

At the Mirror you stare, deep,

at two clear holes, you gaze

You say,

you're ready to take your day.

What a lovely day!

You see?

Happiness is measured through one's

own mean.

Have you, ever told yourself how luck

of you have in?

Have you, ever seen, anyone's shadow

other than the

looks of your own soul?

You don't have this, she got that at ease.

You start complaining, you got nothing.

Then tend to end up grieving.

You start swearing,

you start blaming

Your poor mother,

who drank a glass of water today,

Just to give you chicken you wish for

   today

Your poor diligent father

who's hands wounded to earn a living

for you to wear shoes you wish

for the first day, are you even reading?

You're sick of cars, buses, jeepney, train

You blame the animals , trees, flowers,

   the sun, the moon and rain.

You blame your uncle, your auntie, your

   cousin, friends

classmates, siblings, teachers, the entire

   neighbourhood

you blame the whole world, then the

   good Lord!

Why do you blame them?

What do you call yourself?

45

A Duchess? A Princess? Your Royal
    Highness?
A Prince or Duke or Earl?
A Queen or King?
What a tormented crown!
You blame the whole world saving your
    soul
that has been rotten, before you know.

If you were born without silver in your
    mouth
  then your gotta move
If you were born lucky,
push gratitude.

Life isn't fair, yes indeed, yes it is.
Things happen, thats life, we're uneven.

Monoloquy: Poetry of Inner Voices

It's something human have, that's life,
    that's life.
But that should not be the reason to
    stick,
To stick with twisted philosophies
of you are just you. You are YOU! NOT
    JUST you.
Life isn't measured through great
    achievements.
Great achievements come with great
    pleasure,
with giving the best, and not giving up.
Even failures give you his butt,
just think of things,
that you can do but you are not doing.
Yes, life isn't measured through great
    achievement,
but, imagine things you could have done

But you didn't when you got a lot of

    time?

Time, Time is generous, it gives you

    space to heal.

But speaking of which, where is Time?

Later, tomorrow, day after tomorrow,

a week after next, soon?

Those are future.

Now is Time.

What's the matter? You got your

    necessities

in the 21st Century.

Keep your eyes open, get up,

Stand up.

Remember,

laziness steals Time,

deteriorates wisdom,

it murders soul.

Monoloquy: Poetry of Inner Voices

Shadows of Love

I caught a bird aboard the branch of pouring

    rain.

I held her tight, we shared abode, pro tem.

I fed her all the precious seeds and grain.

She smiled but never flapped her wings the

    same.

I kept her caged, she gave me leash

to tie my neck unto her wings till bleed.

The tighter it is, the more her wings be seized.

I knew she stayed yet never flapped but hid.

I lost her sight, she moved away, I saw

from distant place her eyes were blazing rings.

I took a shot and struck her heart with bow

I saw her flew far off, yet never flapped her
   wings.

Over years apart, I saw her feathered scar.
Her beau as fine as violets in May.
Without the cage I deeply loved her more.
I took the leash then flapped my wings away.

It's when I learned to free her wings.
I saw myself with feathered wings unleashed.
We then ascend the widest seas of poles
with flags of liberty, we're both unseized.

The Best Part

Crystal waters keep us apart,
Strange, but cupid connects our heart
our love is the best part.
Without you life lives in dark.

Black and white would only be
Bound with tears of deepest sea
puzzled patterns we foresee
Only Heart beats for you and me

Wander in Wonderland

Tick! Tock! Tick! Tock!

Mr. Rabbit is anxious again

Tick! Tock! Tick! Tock!

Oh! I've almost forgotten,

the tea party for dear Queen Alice.

The very known,

Alice In Wonderland

Why Alice? Why not Karen?

Karen In Wonderland?

Stephanie? Casey? or perhaps, Jia?

Jia In Wonderland!

How funny will the story might be!

A tea party with Maddy,

Harey and Dormy.

Playing with Deedy, Dumdy,

or with Humpty Dumpy on the wall

or everyone in wonderland!

How funny will the story might be!

I'll wonder off the woods, hills and valleys.

I'll meet Mr. Caterpillar

who smokes cigar.

The Cheshire cat who grinned so big,

instead of him vanishing,

I'll vanish first before him!

How funny will the story might be!

I'll eat breads, muffins and mushrooms,

drink mixtures and juices

to grow small or big, fat or thin!

How funny will the story might be!

If it was me.

Tick! Tock! Tick! Tock!

I see Mr. Rabbit relaxed on his seat

Tick! Tock! Tick! Tock!

Everyone seems to be present

Tick! Tock! Tick! Tock!

Oh dear! Alice and me drinking tea

In Wonderland so full of fun.

Monoloquy: Poetry of Inner Voices

When I was Young

When I was young I used to sit across the lake
Along my selfish mind I ran away
To free from granny's grudge mahogany
Beneath the shady shadow of the tree

I lay and swam the prickling bed of grass,
then picked the flowers weaving crown and
    sash.
I stood and chased the butterflies around,
then glide the hilly tops of mud and sand.

I played around with friends but sometimes
    foe.
We built liaison, cut in times then go,

we ran the itchy fields until we ditched,

we laughed, we cried, until sun turned peach.

Our pupil's wide, our vison black and white.

We had to leave the kingdom for a while,

our limbs were stiff to break our faction,

'twas time of great dramatic separation.

There was my granny waiting at the door,

with magic stick behind,I couldn't see she

   hoard.

When stick caressed my skin my spirit went

away, I knelt on floor, my knees down, bent.

With tears from eyes and nose I swore I won't

come out the castle, I swear, I won't.

It's not a maze but labyrinth that lead

toward the dragon, scammed my head.

57

Constituents had turned the great
spectators.
How valiant, how brave to witness the course!
Their Queen had fallen, dethroned, beheaded,
they did was hid from corner, cold like dead.

When show had ended noodle soup she gave,
my chamber pets went wild I couldn't save
my dignity, the scent was tempting high,
the soup's amazing, I could not lie.

I ate it all with snuffling sound of glee,
then there she went and sit quite next to me.
She stroked my face with towel damp and
   cold,
then down my stinky body rubbed like gold.

She raised my arms with lanes of sour path.

She sniffed the scent, then tickled, I laughed.
She rubbed my back with essence oil like
    cinnamon rolls,
and dressed me garments scent of
    naphthalene balls.

The dragon's tamed as Shakespeare's shrew -
Like child she sipped the coffee freshly
    brewed.
With toasted bread and butter sugary top,
her favourite snack, her heart just hopped.

When I was young, I used to be with granny.
My empty life was filled with joy and glory.
I didn't want to lose I held her hand,
I didn't want the pain I cried like band.

I wish I was with granny until now,

It's hard to figure out the why's and how.

I wish I spent my time than building fake
  realm

I wish I could go back, when I was young.

Wounds

Yes, Rome was not built in a day.
Indeed, Time heals all wounds.
Fake it, conceal it,
but escape never
from its infliction.
Some would fade,
Some wound leave scar.
Amazing, isn't it?
Wounds are mindless, but
envision identity
what kind of scar they give -
a scar which temporarily marks
or scar which permanently lives.
Wounds are eyes
To witness certainty.
To remind humanity.

You Without Me

Fleeting like seeping sand,

we grow up, we realise,

we grow apart, too far.

It hurts, but we learn.

what forever holds is divine quest

it might a concept, timeframe, perhaps

But for never, never

will we let distance cut.

These memories we buried,

Deep, kept, preserved,

For difference is just the absence of

equivalence

But never a forever with you without

me.

Haiku

Sea me now?

Beachin'

I am

Reddish blue night,

Bitter wind strongly whispers:

Teary sky.

Assorted hands tinker:

heads, feet, fingers line up.

Lips move side by side.

Serenity yearning seen from goblet,

overall velvet-textured garb,

Reflecting silhouette falling.

www.ingramcontent.com/pod-product-compliance
Lightning Source LLC
Chambersburg PA
CBHW061259140726
47998CB00006B/2276